The Golden Locket

BY **Carol Greene**

ILLUSTRATED BY **Marcia Sewall**

Harcourt Brace Jovanovich, Publishers

San Diego   New York   London

Requests for permission to make copies of any part of the work should be mailed to:
Permissions Department, Harcourt Brace Jovanovich, Publishers, 8th Floor,
Orlando, Florida 32887.

Library of Congress Cataloging-in-Publication Data
Greene, Carol.
The golden locket/by Carol Greene; illustrated by Marcia Sewall. — 1st ed.
p.   cm.
Summary: Hoping to avoid the worry of caring for a valuable object, Miss Teaberry gives
away the locket her cat finds in the garden, only to find herself enmeshed in a situation of
escalating chaos.
ISBN 0-15-231220-X
[1. Humorous stories.] I. Sewall, Marcia, ill. II. Title.
PZ7.G82845Go   1992   [E]—dc20   90-21788

The illustrations in this book were done in gouache and ink on Fabriano cold-press paper.
The display type was set in Lucian by Thompson Type, San Diego, California.
The text type was set in Della Robbia by Central Graphics, San Diego, California.
Color separations were made by Bright Arts, Ltd., Hong Kong.
Printed and bound by Tien Wah Press, Singapore
Production supervision by Warren Wallerstein and Ginger Boyer
Designed by Lydia D'moch

First edition

A B C D E

For Jordan Cooper
—C. G.

For Bebe, my good kitty
—M. S.

It was all the cat's fault.

For years Miss Teaberry had lived peacefully in her little stone
cottage halfway between two towns. Flowers grew in front of the
cottage and vegetables grew behind. A well on one side gave clear
cold water and an apple tree on the other gave fruit and shade.
   Miss Teaberry had everything she wanted and everything
she needed.

Then one day her cat smelled a mouse beneath the apple tree. He dug and dug. He did not find a mouse. But he did find a golden locket.

He carried it to the front of the cottage where Miss Teaberry had just begun to weed her zinnias.

"Hello, puss, what have you got?" asked Miss Teaberry. She took the locket. "Oh, how fancy!"

Miss Teaberry went inside and put on the locket. It did not look right with her everyday dress.

It did not look right with any of her dresses.

"What a bother!" said Miss Teaberry. "I don't have a dress fancy enough for this locket. And I have wasted the whole day trying on clothes when I meant to weed my zinnias."

She put the locket on the table and made some supper. Then she went to bed. She was almost asleep when she thought of something.

"What a bother!" said Miss Teaberry. "I left the locket on the table. What if a burglar comes in and steals it?"

She jumped out of bed and hurried to the table. On the way, she stubbed her toe. But there lay the locket, safe and sound.

Miss Teaberry took it back to bed with her. On the way, she bumped her head.

"There you are," she said and put the locket under her pillow. "Now you will be safe for sure."

She was almost asleep when she thought of something else. What if the burglar came into her bedroom and took the locket while she was sleeping? She would not like that one bit.

"What a bother!" said Miss Teaberry. "Now I shall have to stay awake all night."

The next morning, Miss Teaberry felt tired and cross. Her toe hurt, and so did her head.

"This locket is nothing but a bother," she declared. "I don't want it and I don't need it. I shall give it away."

Just then the milkman stopped in front of her cottage. Miss Teaberry hurried outside.

"I beg your pardon," she said, "but do you happen to know an enchanting young girl who might like a golden locket?"

The milkman thought for a moment. "There is an enchanting young girl in the town down the road," he said. "I don't think she has a locket."

"Fine!" said Miss Teaberry. "You must take her this one. But do not tell her who it is from. She might want to thank me and that would be a bother. Just say . . . say that the locket is a gift from a secret admirer."

"All right," said the milkman. He drove off, and Miss Teaberry went inside for a long nap.

The next morning the milkman stopped again.

"The enchanting young girl was pleased with the locket," he told Miss Teaberry. "She was so pleased that she wanted to send a return gift to her secret admirer. Here it is."

He set a large basket on the ground. Then he drove off.

"They are purebred and very valuable," he called over his shoulder.

Miss Teaberry opened the basket. Inside were three squirming puppies. "Oh no," said Miss Teaberry.

She spent all day trying to keep the puppies from digging up her zinnias. She spent all night trying to keep them from chewing up her furniture.

The next morning she felt very tired and very cross.

"Please stop!" she called to the milkman, even though it was not her day to get milk. "Do you happen to know a winsome young boy who might like three squirming puppies?"

The milkman thought for a moment. "There is a winsome young boy in the town up the road," he said. "I don't think he has any puppies."

"Fine!" said Miss Teaberry. "You must take him these. Say they are a gift from a secret admirer."

"All right," said the milkman. He drove off, and Miss Teaberry went inside for a long nap.

The next morning the milkman arrived with a large box. Inside was a squawking parrot.

"It's a gift," said the milkman, "from the winsome young boy to his secret admirer."

"Oh no," said Miss Teaberry.

All day the parrot played hide-and-seek with her. All night it sang. It did not sing well.

The next morning Miss Teaberry felt tired and cross indeed.

Once again she stopped the milkman.

"Please take this parrot to the enchanting young girl," she said.

"I know," said the milkman. "Say it is a gift from her secret admirer."

"Right," said Miss Teaberry.

The next day the milkman was back with a dapple-gray horse.

"I know," said Miss Teaberry. "It's a gift from the enchanting young girl."

"Right," said the milkman.

That day the horse ate the tops off her carrots.

That night he ate the apples off her tree.
Miss Teaberry lay awake listening to him crunch.

In the morning she sent him on with the milkman to the winsome young boy.

So it went, day after day.
The winsome young boy sent three playful lambs.

The enchanting young girl sent three plump pigs.

The winsome young boy sent a gaggle of geese.

The enchanting young girl sent a hairy ox with fleas.

Miss Teaberry thought she might go mad. The milkman did not look too well either.

"I am terribly sorry," he said one morning as he squeezed the ox in with his milk bottles. "But this simply must stop."

"I agree," said Miss Teaberry. "You take the ox away and I will try to think of something."

By then she was so tired that it was not easy for her to think. But she held her eyes open until she had an idea. Then she took a long nap.

The next morning she gave the milkman two notes. One was for the enchanting young girl in the town down the road. The other was for the winsome young boy in the town up the road. Both notes said the same thing:

> Please meet me tonight at nine by the apple tree next to the little stone cottage halfway between towns.
>
> — Your secret admirer

Nine o'clock came and Miss Teaberry peeked around the corner of her cottage. There they were—the enchanting young girl and the winsome young boy. Of course they fell in love at once.

Miss Teaberry did not go to the wedding. She stayed home and weeded her zinnias.

But the milkman went and had a splendid time.

So did the cat.

EDUCATION